LALI, LALI! MI FERBUS! *

* HELLO! I'M FERBUS!

£5.50

Edited by Barrie Tomlinson, Creative Editorial Services.

Published by
Grandreams Limited
Jadwin House, 2205/211 Kentish Town Road, London, NW5 2JU.

Printed in Belgium.

TM and ©1996 Saban Entertainment, Inc & Saban International N.V. All Rights Reserved.
Saban's MASKED RIDER and all logos, character names and distinctive likenesses thereof are
trademarks of Saban Entertainment, Inc & Saban International N.V.

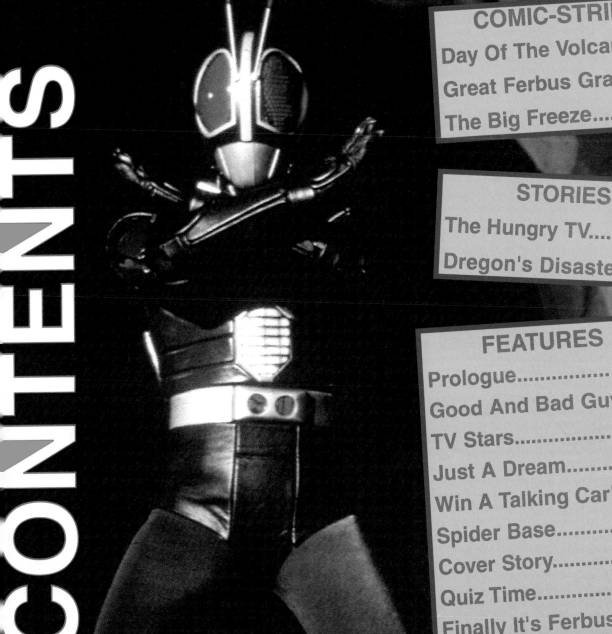

CONTENTS

PROLOGUE...

HOW would you feel if a handsome, teenage alien landed in your back garden, saying he was a super hero from a distant world sent to protect Earth from an evil menace? What would your answer be if this same alien asked if he could move into your home?

This is what happens to the Stewart family when Dex, an alien prince from the distant planet Edenoi, arrives in their lives. Edenoi was once a place of peace, but it had become a world of chaos because of the evil Count Dregon. Banished from Edenoi many years before, Dregon aimed to get his revenge by enslaving the people of the planet.

As his world faced defeat, King Lexian, ruler of Edenoi, discovered that Earth was the next target for Count Dregon. The King sent his grandson Dex, Prince of Edenoi, across millions of miles of space to protect our planet. Although it may have been too late to save Edenoi, the King believed Dex could still foil Dregon's plans to destroy the Earth.

Before leaving Edenoi, King Lexian gave Dex special powers - the powers of the Masked Rider!

When danger threatens, Dex transforms into an insect-like super hero with amazing strength, incredible powers, awesome weapons and fantastic vehicles.

The Masked Rider's two space-age, computer programmed vehicles are Combat Chopper, a bug-eyed talking motorbike, and Magno, a turbo-charged talking car. Together they're unbeatable!

Count Dregon wears a golden mask which hides his hideous face, scarred in battle with King Lexian. Dregon has sworn vengeance against Dex and his family. He also believes the powers of the Masked Rider should be his.

Known as the head honcho of hatred, Dregon is twisted, corrupt, conceited and lethal. With an army of ruthless robots and atrocious aliens to call upon, he knows only one thing stands between him and the conquest of Earth - the Masked Rider!

On Earth, Dex lives with the Stewart family, the only humans who know he is the Masked Rider. Hal Stewart runs a TV repair shop from his garage. His wife, Barbara Stewart, has her own catering business. Their adopted children are fifteen-year old Molly and ten-year old Albee.

Dex finds it difficult to settle into Earth life at home and at school. Earth is very different to Edenoi! The Masked Rider has one friend from his home planet with him. This is Ferbus, Dex's fur ball alien pet. The lovable animal is always getting into trouble and Dex has to rescue him!

Count Dregon's headquarters is Spider Base. From there, Dregon sends out giant, bug-like robots, Insectivores, to cause chaos and destruction. The Masked Rider's mission is to defeat them and the rest of Dregon's bizarre followers. These include an evil sorceress known as Nefaria, an alien general called Double Face, a one-eyed robot named Cyclopter and Gork, a goat-like alien life form that Dregon keeps around for laughs.

Other dangers the Masked Rider comes up against include the Maggots, Nefaria's multi-coloured insect henchmen, as well as sinister Skull Reapers and creepy Commandoids. With so many creatures and robots matched against the Masked Rider, he has to use all his super strength and super powers to beat them. When not protecting the Earth, Dex has to guard the Stewart family and his pet Ferbus. It's a tough job for even the Masked Rider!

ENOUGH OF THIS HISTORY LESSON! GET ON WITH THE ANNUAL! I, COUNT DREGON, WILL SHOW YOU HOW QUICKLY I DEAL WITH THE MASKED RIDER!

DAY OF THE VOLCANO!

INTRODUCING...
THE HERO!

DO you know what Dex says when he summons the special, out-of-this-world powers of the Masked Rider? "Ectophase Activate!" Seconds later the insect-like super hero is ready for action. When wearing his famous Masked Rider outfit, above left, the alien prince from Edenoi uses an amazing sword called the Electro Saber. On the right above is Masked Rider in his Super Gold outfit. Masked Rider Super Gold rides the Super Chopper motorbike and he has a powerful laser pistol called the Ectoray to use against those baddest of bad guys! Talking of villains, read the notice below!

CAUTION! THE VILLAINS ARE ON THE NEXT TWO PAGES!

THE VILLAINS!

PROBABLY the baddest bad guy in the whole universe...and certainly the most dangerous, Count Dregon holds a terrible grudge after being banished from his home planet, Edenoi, years ago. As an act of revenge, Dregon caused untold suffering and destruction on his own world. Now the Earth is next in line for demolition. Dregon has created a mighty army of robotic insects, the Insectivores, to do his bidding. The creatures are kept in special glass tubes deep inside the Count's Spider Base headquarters. When launching another deadly assault on our planet, Dregon places one of the glass tubes in a vacuum tube and fires it at the latest target. The Insectivore becomes full sized once on Earth and is ready to cause as much chaos as possible. It's up to the Masked Rider to defeat the Insectivores and wreck all of Count Dregon's evil plans!

Count Dregon has a whole army of dodgy characters to send into battle against the Masked Rider. Cyclopter, above left, is a one-eyed alien robot. Totally loyal to his master, Cyclopter enjoys beating any opponent who is foolish enough to stand in his way. He is a real tough 'guy'- a sort of Clint Eastwood in a robot outfit! Shown at top right is Double Face, a really weird, two-faced alien general. Double Face keeps Dregon's operations running, using ruthless military control. Nefaria, also pictured on this page, is the beautiful, but evil, alien sorceress. She is the favourite of Count Dregon and he listens to her more than any of his other fiendish followers. Easily recognised by the yellow feather in her hat, Nefaria is often called 'The Lady Macbeth' of the Spider Base. This scheming character is one to avoid!

THE HUNGRY TV!

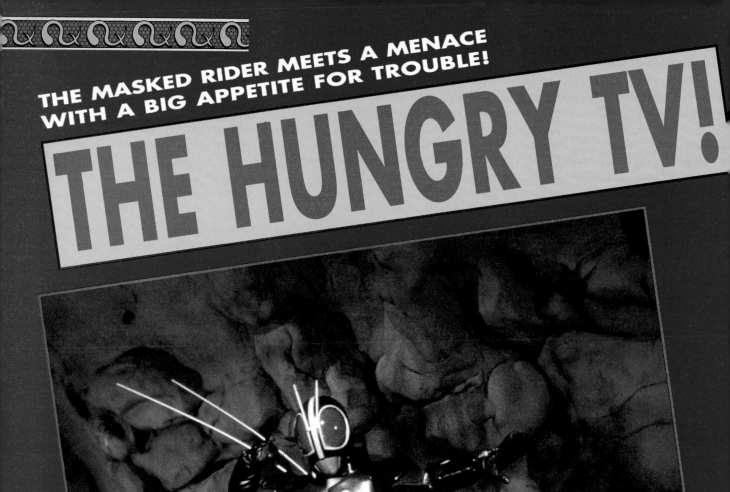

RAIN hammered against the windows of the Stewart house. The wind howled around outside the building like some monstrous wild animal.

Every few seconds a flash of lightning lit up the night sky.

The deep rumble of thunder increased in volume as the storm grew ever closer.

Hal Stewart was tinkering with his latest invention, a highly advanced and rapid speed machine for making French fries.

Unfortunately, all it had produced so far were some

soggy lumps of uneatable mush.

Vowing to solve the problem, Hal had dismantled his invention on the kitchen table. Bits and pieces were everywhere. It looked like some giant mechanical jigsaw puzzle.

Occasionally, he would pick

a piece up, tinker with it for a few moments and then return it to the mini-junk yard in front of him.

"Totally useless machine," Hal Stewart muttered under his breath. "Stop messing me around and start working. Do you hear me? W-O-R-K!"

His wife, Barbara Stewart, smiled and shook her head. She knew better than to get involved in her husband's crazy inventions.

Barbara had just made a cake. A chocolate cake. Only the chocolate cake was not where she had left it. It had vanished!

Molly and Albee Stewart were sitting in front of the TV with Dex, watching cartoons.

Dex frowned as he watched a brightly coloured, talking crocodile chase an equally brightly coloured, talking anteater up the side of a skyscraper.

"Why?" Dex asked in a confused voice.

Ten-year old Albee Stewart laughed. Molly Stewart smiled. Aliens from distant planets asked really dumb questions!

Only Dex's adopted family knew that he was really a prince of the planet Edenoi, sent to Earth to protect our world from the menace of Count Dregon.

A prince who possessed the most awesome powers of the Masked Rider!

Suddenly, a knocking began at the front door. Except that it was a very strange sort of knocking. Three or four seconds passed between each separate sound.

"Who can that be at this time of night?" asked Hal Stewart

as he went to answer the door.

The door creaked long and loudly as it was opened. Hal winced. He had been meaning to oil the hinges for months.

Hal Stewart stared outside into the dark and stormy night. Then he heard a noise behind him. He turned and let out a surprised cry.

Barbara, Dex, Molly and Albee were standing right behind him!

"Don't sneak up on me like that, guys!" gasped Hal, trying to get his breath back.

The entire Stewart family strained their eyes and gazed out into the gloom. There was

no-one there. Just shadows.

Then one of the shadows moved as a flash of lightning lit up the scene.

"Good evening," the woman began in a strange, high pitched voice. "I understand you run a TV repair shop here...?"

The speaker wore black gloves, with a long black cloak which reached almost to the ground. A large, black hat sat on her head.

Long blonde hair reached almost to her waist. One eye was covered by a black eye-patch.

"Y-Yes," stammered Hal Stewart after a long pause. "What do you want repaired?"

The strange woman stood to one side and indicated a portable television set. It was sitting in a wheelbarrow.

"The repair will probably take a day or so," explained Hal Stewart to the woman. "Do you want to leave your telephone number...?"

"I shall return tomorrow," she replied. "Farewell!"

Before Hal could say anything, the mystery woman had vanished into the storm. A relieved Mr. Stewart brought in the television and shut the front door.

"Now that," said Barbara Stewart, "was the strangest

visitor we've ever had here!"

Albee laughed. "Apart from Dex that is!"

Dex picked Albee up by his feet and held him high in the air. It was a simple task for someone with the strength of the Masked Rider!

"Strange am I?" smiled Dex as he carried the giggling Albee around the room. "Not as strange as going about

the house upside down!"

Hal Stewart decided it was too late to make a start on repairing the TV. He took the set to his repair shop in the garage.

As Hal turned off the light and closed the door, he failed to notice a pair of sinister eyes glaring at him from the screen of the TV.

Outside in the rain, the

Stewarts' female visitor pulled off her disguise of a fake eye-patch, blonde wig, gloves, hat and cloak.

She did not seem to care that she was now getting very wet.

"Hee-hee!" cackled Nefaria, (for it was she!) Count Dregon's scheming second-in-command, as she boarded a powerful black motorbike.

"Mission accomplished. The

Stewarts are in for a nasty surprise!"

Albee Stewart was the first up the following morning. There were a whole bunch of strange noises coming from the garage where Albee's father had his TV repair shop.

Albee opened the door and looked inside the garage.

What appeared to be a living TV set was running around the garage. It had a hideous face with glaring eyes and big teeth. Legs with long claws came from the base of the TV.

All other television sets had been destroyed. Most were in little pieces. Some had even been half eaten!

"Oh, boy!" said Albee. "You'll be in real trouble when Dad sees this mess!"

The living TV paused for a second and stared at the youngest member of the Stewart family. Then it charged.

Now even though Albee was only ten years old, he knew this was the time to make a fast exit!

Albee raced out of the garage faster than Carl Lewis. He slammed the door behind him and leaned against it, puffing heavily.

Then Albee heard a noise. The noise of wood being eaten by big teeth.

"HEEEEELLLLLLLLP!" screamed Albee at the top of his voice.

Hearing the desperate cry for assistance, Dex transformed himself into his secret, super hero identity - as the Masked Rider!

As the ravenous television ate right through the garage door, Masked Rider launched himself into the air.

"Leave Albee alone!" roared the super hero from Edenoi, as he sent the TV flying across the room with a devastating Rider Kick.

CRASH! The hungry horror collided with the kitchen wall.

THUMP! The alive TV hit the washing machine.

WHAM! The set bounced off the kitchen table.

THE HUNGRY TV
Continuation...

The rest of the Stewart family joined Albee as they watched the amazing contest between an alien prince and the terrible TV.

Like bizarre wrestlers, the fighting duo were rolling around the kitchen floor. The gnashing teeth of the gruesome television were going for the Masked Rider's throat.

"Oh, no, you don't," gasped the hero from Edenoi. "I'm switching you off for good!"

Using all his super strength, the Masked Rider hurled the televisual menace upwards. It smashed into the ceiling and shattered into a thousand pieces.

"Look out! It's raining bits of TV!" warned Hal Stewart.

Everyone moved just fast enough to avoid the falling debris. The Stewart family helped Dex, in his guise as the Masked Rider, to his feet.

"I know watching too much TV is meant to be bad for you," said a grim faced Molly, "but this is crazy!"

Dex dusted down his Masked Rider outfit. "That was the set that woman brought round last night!"

"I thought there was something funny about her!" replied Hal Stewart.

"Whatever gave you that idea, Hal!" laughed Barbara Stewart.

Dex was sure the evil Count Dregon must be behind this.

He was proved right within seconds. The Stewarts' house was surrounded by a trio of nasty looking insect-like creatures, which proceeded to attack the building.

"Maggots!" Dex warned as he looked through the window. "They must think their friend the TV beat me!"

Concentrating hard, Dex began using his Masked Rider's special telepathic powers. His mind sent an urgent message calling for assistance.

The Stewarts' house began to shake. There was the sound of breaking glass and splintering wood. The three Maggots were forcing their way inside!

A scared Albee flung his arms around Hal Stewart and clung to him tightly.

"Do something, Dad!" cried the young boy.

"Only the Masked Rider can save us now, son!" answered a grim Mr. Stewart.

"With a little help from my friends of course," laughed Dex. "Magno and Chopper just arrived!"

Summoned by their master's telepathic powers, the talking car and talking motorbike screeched to a halt outside the Stewarts' house.

Dex knew Dregon's insect-like henchmen were after him alone. He would lead them away from his adopted human family.

Racing out of the house at super speed, Dex shoulder charged his way through the Maggots and then jumped into Magno's driving seat.

"Hi, Dex," the talking car greeted him. "Nice day for a drive."

"Cut the chat and hit the gas!" shouted the Masked Rider in reply.

Magno started to move, but a split second too late. The trio of Maggots leapt on the outside of the vehicle and clung on as the car increased speed.

"Hey, Magno!" chuckled the following Chopper talking motorbike. "Seems as though you've picked up some hitchhikers!"

Magno said nothing in reply, increasing speed and zig-zagging across the road in an attempt to shake off the Maggots.

All to no avail. The creatures held on, crawling closer and closer to the Masked Rider!

Dex knew he had to act fast. A series of rapid instructions were given to Magno: left, right, left again, another right then...

"Turn into the gas station! Don't stop! Go straight on into the car wash!"

Magno ended up gleaming clean and minus Maggots.

"Most excellent," said a pleased Dex. "That got rid of the surplus weight!"

"Hey, buddy!" called the gas station attendant. "Do these belong to you?"

The attendant was pointing at a great, soaking wet, soapy mass of Maggots lying at the end of the car wash.

"Send them back to Count Dregon at Spider Base!" came the laughing reply from the rapidly speeding away Magno.

The Stewart family were answering their front door to a caller - a very familiar caller!

"Good morning," said the strange woman with the high pitched voice. "I have returned to collect the television I left for repair."

Hal Stewart caught his breath. His eyes narrowed. It was the same blonde haired woman with the eye-patch who had called the previous night.

"Just a second," fumed Mr. Stewart. "I'll get the set for you!"

Hal returned with a large cardboard box which he tipped out in front of the weird woman. A great pile of broken television parts landed at her feet.

The woman's jaw dropped open in stunned surprise. For almost a minute she didn't say a word.

"Curse you!" screamed Nefaria, throwing off her disguise. "You should all have ended up as TV dinners!"

SLAM! The door crashed shut in Nefaria's face, leaving her with a very sore nose. Count Dregon's number two ranted and raved, kicking and punching the door.

"How dare you shut me out! I'm a very important villainess!

I'll make you pay for this! Just you wait!"

Ferbus, Dex's fur ball alien pet, had just finished eating Barbara Stewarts' missing chocolate cake in some nearby bushes.

Ferbus saw what had happened between Nefaria and the Stewart family. He did not like nasty people threatening his human friends.

The Masked Rider, Magno and Chopper arrived back to see an amazing sight: Count Dregon's cohort Nefaria being chased away by Ferbus!

"EEEEEK!" shrieked Nefaria. "Get away! Leave me alone!"

Then everything seemed to happen at once: Poor Ferbus tripped over and fell flat on his face, Magno swerved to avoid the fur ball and hit a tree and Nefaria jumped aboard her powerful black motorbike to make her escape while the going was good.

"Ferbus!" cried a very worried Masked Rider. "Are you okay?"

The fur ball was sitting on the ground, rubbing a sore nose. There were a lot of sore noses around today!

"Dokey okey, Dex," replied the Masked Rider's pet.

Ferbus pointed after the rapidly disappearing Nefaria and the animal's meaning was obvious: Go get her!

"Damage report, Magno?" asked the concerned Dex of his talking car.

"Minor only, Dex," confirmed the vehicle, "but the tree is a write-off!"

Magno raced away in a great cloud of smoke and burnt rubber, with Chopper close behind. The chase was on!

The pursuit went on for mile after mile. Through city and country. Over mountains and plains. Through tunnels and across bridges. Past great forests and lakes. No quarter was given. Nor asked for.

"This has gone on long enough, Magno!" called Dex at last. "Slow Nefaria down with a blast of your energy beam!"

"Spoilsport!" moaned the talking car. "I was really enjoying this chase!"

ZAP! Magno's powerful energy beam sliced the bridge Nefaria was crossing in half.

"OH, NOOOOOO!" screamed the falling sorceress as she landed in the river below with a giant splash.

Being a good guy, the Masked Rider stopped Magno

to check Nefaria was okay.

As Dex got out of his talking car, a giant shadow fell across him. He had been led into a trap! An Insectivore, a huge robot wasp, swooped down on the Masked Rider. Riding on the back of the machine was the bad guy called Cyclopter.

Caught in the open, Dex knew he had to fight back hard and fast. Drawing his powerful sword, he struck out at the diving Insectivore.

"Electro Saber activate! You're going down, Mr. Nasty Cyclopter!"

The first swing of the sword neatly removed one of the flying robot's metal legs. The second took a great chunk out of the machine's body. The third missed completely - and the Electro Saber was knocked from the Masked Rider's grasp!

"Now I'm in mega trouble!" cried a grim Dex. "My only chance is to reach Magno or Chopper!"

It was too late. The Insectivore swooped down

THE HUNGRY TV Continuation...

and snatched Dex off the ground.

"Return the prisoner to Spider Base at maximum speed," Cyclopter ordered the Insectivore. "Nefaria and I will follow in Magno and Chopper!"

"Go along with the bad guys for the moment," Dex whispered to his talking vehicles using his wrist communicator, "while I figure how to get out of this!"

The talking vehicles obeyed, doing nothing as Count Dregon's followers boarded them.

They allowed the sinister duo to think they were driving them. In reality Magno and Chopper were in control!

The Insectivore set course for Spider Base carrying its struggling passenger.

A desperate Dex used his Masked Rider's X-ray vision to scan the machine, searching for a weak spot somewhere on the robotic bug.

He found one! A powerful punch tore a hole in the Insectivore's outer skin. Dex then reached inside and grabbed a whole bunch of vital internal wiring.

A swift tug and an explosion of electrical sparks followed. The doomed Insectivore rolled on to its back and started to dive towards the ground.

"Chopper! Ditch your bad guy passenger now!" Dex ordered urgently.

It was time for Cyclopter and Nefaria to get what they deserved!

A rapid burst of acceleration by the talking motorbike caught Cyclopter totally by surprise.

The helpless alien lost his balance and plunged off the machine landing in the middle of the biggest and smelliest compost heap for miles!

"GLUURRGGH!" spluttered the disgusted Cyclopter.

The Insectivore hurtled downwards, trailing a great cloud of smoke and flame. At the last second, the Masked Rider jumped clear and dropped neatly into the seat of his waiting Chopper bike.

KAABOOM! The Insectivore smashed into the ground, exploding in a great ball of heat and flame.

"Time to lose Nefaria, Magno!" Dex ordered the talking car.

Almost before the Masked Rider finished speaking, there was a great explosion of sound from Magno. A secret ejection seat had fired.

"Help!" cried Dregon's number two as she was propelled high into the sky.

"What a relief!" she gasped as a parachute sprang open above her.

Her relief quickly evaporated when she saw where she was about to land: The local duck pond!

SPLOOSH! Nefaria plunged into the dark, murky depths, scattering the ducks in all directions.

The soaking wet Nefaria crawled out of the water just as the very smelly Cyclopter walked up. Neither was looking forward to arriving at Spider Base first to tell Count Dregon the latest bad news.

"After you, Cyclopter!" offered Nefaria.

"No, after you, Nefaria!" insisted Cyclopter.

Dex smiled and set course for the Stewart house. It was time to go home.

All the Stewart family were waiting to welcome back Dex: Hal, Barbara, Molly, Albee and, waving from behind a tree, Ferbus. They were all eating French Fries!

"Way to go, Dex," cried Hal Stewart. "Count Dregon's plans ended up in the trash again!"

"I did have some assistance from Magno and Chopper!" replied a grinning Masked Rider. "I could never have done it without their help!"

Magno and Chopper revved their engines in a totally embarrassed manner.

If they could have blushed they would have done!

TV STARS!

THERE'S a fine line-up of acting talent in the popular new television series that features the Masked Rider.

That's the whole of the Stewart family in the photograph at the top of the page. On the next few pages we'll be introducing you to these actors and actresses who help bring the excitement of the Masked Rider to our screens.

But first of all...watch out! That looks like nasty Count Dregon's creepy, insect-like followers on the right - the Maggots! Who invited them to this article on TV stars? Sorry, guys...this feature is all about folk who look human!

HAL AND BARBARA STEWART

It's time to meet the stars of the Masked Rider TV series! Hal and Barbara Stewart are shown in the above picture. Hal Stewart is played by David Stenstrom, an actor who has appeared in many TV series and feature films. He has also done considerable work in the theatre. David also enjoys singing, playing musical instruments, improvisation and horseback riding!

Candace Camille Bender is the actress who appears as Barbara Stewart. Born in Southern California, Candace lived in London for a time. Before deciding on an acting career, she worked for a while as a professional clown. Apart from her TV and film work, Candace enjoys playing the flute, dancing, juggling and practising her karate!

On the right is one of the Stewarts' adopted children, ten year old Albee. Ashton J. McArn (AJ) plays the part of Dex's number one fan. AJ was born in Fresno, California and he is the youngest of six brothers and sisters. After starting acting in school plays, AJ moved on to commercials and TV series. He likes playing basketball, football and baseball as well as going to the cinema and playing video games!

ALBEE STEWART

MOLLY STEWART

MOLLY and ALBEE

Molly Stewart, Hal and Barbara's fifteen-year old adopted daughter, is played by Rheannon Glover. Born in Southern California, Rheannon started on the road to fame and fortune by appearing in beauty contests at the age of five. She loves ballet, jazz and tap-dancing as well as horse riding and swimming. Oh-oh! What have Molly and Albee seen in the picture on the right? One of Dregon's horrible Insectivores? Better call for the Masked Rider!

29

DEX (MASKED RIDER)

TJ Roberts is the handsome teenage actor who plays the part of Dex, the Masked Rider! Ted Jan Roberts (he prefers being called TJ!) was born on September 24, 1979, in San Diego, California. Martial arts were a fave of this brilliant athlete from an early age. Amazingly, TJ became a black belt in the martial art of Tae Kwon Do at the age of eleven! In 1992, the Roberts' family moved to Los Angeles so that TJ could follow his dream of an acting career. Being so close to Hollywood was a smart move, as TJ soon gained parts in TV series and films. TJ says he and Dex are alike in a lot of ways - except, of course, that he is an Earthling!

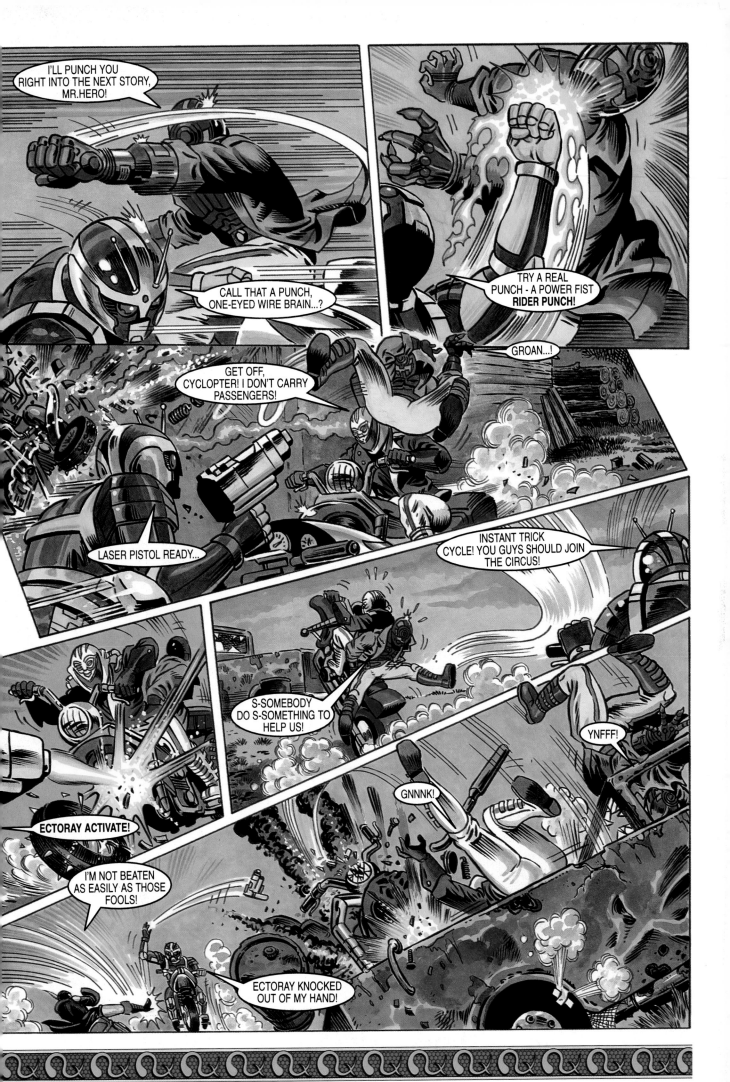

JUST A DREAM!

OR WAS IT?

VROOOOOM! The Masked Rider, on his Combat Chopper motorbike, was in hot pursuit of the robot, Cyclopter!

A sudden ambush! Count Dregon's alien forces were closing in!

"Jack! That's enough playing with your toys! Time for bed!"

Ten year old Jack Johnson sighed. "Oh, Mum! Just a few more minutes - the bad guys have the Masked Rider trapped!"

Mrs Johnson was having none of it. "Bed, young man. The Masked Rider will have to hold out until tomorrow."

Jack sadly put his Masked Rider figures and vehicles away.

The youngster was tired. Five minutes later he

"Welcome aboard, new recruit!" said the talking car.

"Wow! I can't believe this is happening!" gasped an amazed Jack, as Magno raced away at incredible speed.

The Masked Rider explained that Combat Chopper had been captured by Count Dregon. The alien nasty meant to melt down the talking motorbike.

"No way!" shouted a determined Jack.

Magno screeched around a corner and raced up a muddy road towards an old farm.

"That farm is Dregon's hideout!" announced the Masked Rider.

Jack felt they were being watched.

PTOOOOM! As they passed a barn, it was blown apart. It was the nearest of near misses!

"Keep down! We're being fired on!" warned Dex.

Cyclopter was charging towards them, all guns blazing, on his dangerous Cannon Wheels motorbike.

Someone needed to think of a plan fast. That

was in bed fast asleep.

"Wake up! Can you hear me? Wake up!"

Someone was shaking Jack's shoulder.

"Who is it?" he asked sleepily.

"The name's Dex, my friend, but you know me better as the..."

"...Masked Rider!" cried the excited boy, rapidly waking up.

The prince from the distant planet Edenoi told Jack there was no time to waste. He needed help urgently!

Jack jumped out of his bed at record speed. "Ready for duty, Masked Rider!"

"Then come with me!" shouted Dex as they raced out of the house.

Waiting outside, engine running, was the razor-backed car called Magno. It was just like the toy car Jack had been playing with!

The super hero told Jack to jump in as he himself leapt behind the wheel.

someone was Jack. He thought very fast!

Many times before he had helped the Masked Rider defeat Cyclopter, when playing with his toys. Now he knew exactly what to do!

"Drive through that puddle at maximum speed!" he ordered.

The talking car did just that. A great wave of muddy water cascaded over Cyclopter.

"There's mud in your eye, bad guy!" laughed Dex.

"I can't see!" wailed Dregon's robotic minion.

KA-BOOOM! The out of control motorbike collided with a farm tractor and exploded, blowing Cyclopter high in the air.

"EEEEEK!" cried the alien robot. "Where's my parachute?"

"Look out!" warned the eagle-eyed Jack. "More bad guys heading our way: Double Face, Skull Reaper and Robosect!"

"Those three are always big trouble in my toy collection!" said Jack.

Magno was totally surrounded.

"Any ideas, buddy?" asked the Masked Rider.

Jack grinned. "Yes. Slow down and stop, Magno!"

As soon as the car stopped, the terrible trio jumped aboard. Just as Jack had planned!

"Full speed ahead, Magno! Drive through the pig sty!" Jack instructed.

The talking car obeyed. None of the bad guys could hold on.

SPLOOSH! They landed up to their necks in...yuk!

Dex laughed. "A most excellent move. Just Dregon to go now!"

Jack spotted the chief baddie. He was making his escape in a rusty old van. Count Dregon didn't usually leave Spider Base but on this occasion he had! The van was towing a trailer, in which Combat Chopper was secured with heavy chains.

"Help me!" cried the talking motorbike.

Jack knew they had to move fast. "Come up alongside Dregon, Magno!"

The talking car did as he was told.

"Now, Dex!" shouted Jack. "Use your Electro Saber!"

Swinging the sword-like weapon, the Masked Rider sliced through the metal arm linking the van and trailer.

Dregon looked back and saw he had lost Combat Chopper.

Taking his eyes off the road was a mistake.

The van crashed through a fence and overturned in a field, which had a big sign: 'BEWARE OF THE BULL!'

This bull did not like strangers in his field. Especially strangers with gold heads. Dregon was chased over the hills and far away.

Combat Chopper was free again. The Masked Rider turned to his young ally.

"A million thanks. We'd never have beaten Dregon without your help!"

"Time for you to get up, Jack!" called Mrs Johnson.

It was morning. Jack was back home in bed.

The youngster sighed. "It must all have been a dream!"

Then Jack saw a note nearby.

The note said: 'TO JACK, MANY THANKS AGAIN FOR ALL YOUR HELP. ENJOY YOUR PRESENT! THE MASKED RIDER.'

By his bed was a new toy - Masked Rider in his Super Gold outfit!

Jack gulped.

Maybe, just sometimes, dreams can come true!

THE sinister alien craft known as Spider Base was hidden deep in the gloomy depths of a dark forest.

Inside the main control room, the bitter and twisted Count Dregon had called his fiendish followers to a meeting.

Cyclopter, Nefaria, Double Face and Gork were reporting on their latest missions against the hated Masked Rider.

Dregon was in a good mood. He enjoyed being a nasty and horrible alien tyrant.

The Count settled back in his chair and prepared to be entertained with tales of Masked Rider defeats. Or so he thought.

"Begin!" commanded the chief bad guy.

Nefaria, the evil sorceress, spoke first. "The miserable Masked Rider attends Leawood High School in his human guise as Dex. Using my cunning powers of disguise, I became a school inspector and entered that academic atrocity..."

Things started well, Nefaria explained. She was able to move freely around Leawood High with no-one suspecting her true identity.

"Do you know a boy called Dex?" Nefaria slyly questioned

one member of staff.

The teacher smiled. "He's one of our best students and a superb athlete who has been selected for the school swimming squad!"

Further investigation by Count Dregon's cohort revealed that Dex was swimming first in a competition against another school the following day.

It was an opportunity not to be missed. That night, Nefaria sneaked quietly into the school leading the trio of insect creatures known as Maggots.

Quietly? Maybe not!

CRASH! BUMP! THUD!

"You fools!" hissed Nefaria. "Are you trying to get caught?"

The Maggots shook their heads. They lay in a tangled heap on the floor, after tripping over each other and falling down some stairs.

Finding a more clumsy trio of alien creatures would be very difficult.

Nefaria began to spell out the details of her perfect (or so she thought) plan as the Maggots fell in line behind her.

"When Dex dives into the pool, you grab him. Then carry the Masked Rider back to Spider Base at top speed.

"Nothing can go wrong!" Nefaria continued confidently. "Not even you Maggots can fail

this time...Maggots?"

She stopped and looked around. The corridor was empty. Where had they gone?

A light was on in a nearby classroom. Nefaria hurried over.

Two Maggots were seated at desks, noisily eating pages from various school books. Then they started eating the desks themselves. Equally noisily.

The third Maggot was obviously the teacher. The creature was scrawling on the blackboard with a piece of chalk.

Then it started to eat the chalk. With the blackboard as dessert!

"Disgusting!" scolded Nefaria. "I've told you not to snack between meals!"

The Maggots trooped out of the classroom like naughty schoolboys.

This time Nefaria took no chances. She made the moaning and mumbling Maggots walk in front of her.

Eventually, they reached the locked doors of the swimming pool block. Nefaria zapped the doors with a high power laser shot.

"Now get inside, hide in the pool and wait in ambush for the Masked Rider!" she commanded.

Nefaria sealed the doors with another laser shot and smiled. "Poor Dex! This time tomorrow he'll be a prisoner in Spider Base!"

DREGON'S

THE BAD GUY'S BAD GUYS PROVE TACKLING THE MASKED RIDER ISN'T THAT EASY!

DISASTERS!

SABAN's MASKED RIDER

DREGON'S DISASTERS!
Continuation...

Dregon cackled happily as Nefaria paused making her report. "Everything was on course for the capture of the Masked Rider! Surely nothing could go wrong?"

The sorceress suddenly turned very pale and nervous. "Listen to what happened next..."

Next morning, Nefaria hid in the shadows outside the swimming pool waiting for the competition to start.

Things seemed very quiet.

Two men eventually arrived. They wore bright pink overalls with POOL MAINTENANCE on their backs.

Both men had their names on their breast pockets. Strangely, both names were 'Bob'.

"Just look at that, Bob," groaned Bob. "Someone's stolen the 'closed for maintenance' sign again!"

"Shocking, Bob," said the other Bob. "It's lucky everyone knew the swimming competition was being held at that other school..."

A loud bump made the two men called Bob turn round. A school inspector had fainted. They wondered why.

Then the maintenance men heard some strange noises coming from the swimming pool.

"Someone's in the pool Bob!" said Bob.

"Why? There's no water in there!" answered Bob.

The Bobs hurried to the side of the bone dry swimming pool. Staring up at them were the unhappy Maggots.

"EEEEEEK!" cried Bob. "Call the pest exterminator!"

"EEEEEEK!" cried the three Maggots.

Nefaria finished her report in Spider Base. She looked embarrassed. Count Dregon was banging his metal head on the table.

"What a disaster - and to make matters worse, Dex won the swimming competition!"

The Count turned to Double Face who was scratching nervously at his tiny white face.

"Your turn, Double Face! Mak your report - and it had bett be a good one!"

The strangest of alie generals made a nervou swallowing noise and began t speak.

"I bravely went undercove with a force of Skull Reapers t capture the Masked Rider..."

Double Face explained that and the Skull Reapers ha disguised themselves as fak police officers. They wore fak uniforms and drove equally fak patrol cars.

"Heh-heh!" cackled a Sku Reaper. "We're the cops. Wher are the robbers?"

Double Face resisted th temptation to vaporise hi foolish follower. Although on just.

Working quickly, the fake cop set up a roadblock on the edg of town. They knew the Maske Rider would pass that wa sooner or later.

It was later. Three weeks late to be exact.

By this time, half the Sku Reapers had deserted. Two fak police cars had been stolen Another four had all their wheel stolen.

99,999 vehicles had passe through the roadblock.

Then a warning cry went up The talking car called Magn was approaching!

Dex, at the wheel of Magno i his super hero guise as th Masked Rider, was puzzled as h saw the roadblock ahead.

"Strange!" stated Dex."Thos cops look like Double Face an some Skull Reapers!"

"Maybe that's because it i Double Face and some Skul Reapers!" replied Magno.

The talking car slowed as approached the roadblock.

They joined the queue o vehicles behind a stagecoach, space shuttle transporter and motorised pogo-stick.

Dex and Magno soon reache the front of the queue. Double Face, wearing an ill-fitting police sergeant's uniform, was waiting

"Who are you?" barked the disguised alien general.

"The Masked Rider, prince of the planet Edenoi an well-known super hero!" Dex

answered.

Double Face just stopped himself jumping into the air and shouting 'At last! Yahoooo!'

"This won't take a moment, sir. Please get out of the car!" instructed the bad guy.

Dex grinned behind his mask. "I would obey, officer - but I recognise your faces, Double Face!"

VROOOOOM! Magno hit the gas and ran right over the alien general's foot.

"YEE-OOOWWW!" he wailed.

Magno smashed through the roadblock, sending fake cop cars and fake cops flying in all directions.

The bad guys jumped in their cars and gave high speed chase. Within seconds the fast moving Magno was boxed in and totally surrounded by the enemy.

Dregon loudly interrupted Double Face's story inside Spider Base.

"Don't tell me the Masked Rider managed to escape from that impossible situation!"

Double Face was on his feet and hurrying towards the exit.

"Excuse me, boss! I just remembered a very urgent appointment - on Mars!"

Dregon leapt to his feet and yelled at the top of his voice: "COME BACK AND FINISH YOUR REPORT!"

A resigned Double Face did exactly as he had been told.

The rest of his story was enough to make a grown bad guy cry.

DREGON'S DISASTERS!
Continuation...

ZAP! A powerful energy beam fired from Magno cut one chasing car in half. The two halves went in different directions, a helpless Skull Reaper in each.

One down. Five to go.

KERUMP! A cloud of dust thrown up by Magno made the Skull Reapers in the car behind cough and splutter. Unable to see, they crashed into a haystack.

Two down. Four to go.

CRASH! Dex activated his Electro Saber and used the sword-like weapon to puncture a front wheel as another car came alongside. The vehicle skidded and overturned.

Three down. Three to go.

SMASH! Magno slowed, then speeded up. Two opposition cars charging in could not stop in time and collided.

Five down. One to go.

BUMP! Double Face's vehicle rammed Magno from behind.

KERUNCH! The powerful talking car went into reverse. Double Face jumped clear as his car was pushed hard into a wall and crushed almost flat.

Six down. Zero to go!

The Masked Rider and Magno vanished in a speeding cloud of dust.

Double Face ditched his fake uniform and ran. He heard the sound of approaching police sirens.

Real police sirens!

It was every bad guy for himself. The Skull Reapers would have to look after themselves!

Count Dregon shook with fury as Double Face completed his report in Spider Base.

"You two faced fool! The Masked Rider got away and all the Skull Reapers were arrested!"

Dregon picked up his chair and hurled it angrily at the wall. Bits flew all over the place. One hit the Count, denting his gold face.

"Look what you've done now!" screeched Dregon, rubbing his damaged metal head.

Double Face cowered under his own chair.

"D-don't hurt me!" he wailed. "Have mercy on this miserable being!"

Dregon turned away from the failed alien general and jabbed a finger at the goat-like alien life form known as Gork.

"Your turn! Tell me how your plan went!"

The bizarre creature began to speak in a weird kind of alien rhyme.

"Masked Rider's birthday it was not, but I sent him a present he had not got..."

Gork explained that one of Dregon's biggest and nastiest Insectivores was a giant locust.

He had wrapped the bad tempered robot in brown paper and string, then sent the parcel to the Stewart family.

The Stewarts were the humans the Masked Rider lived with on Earth.

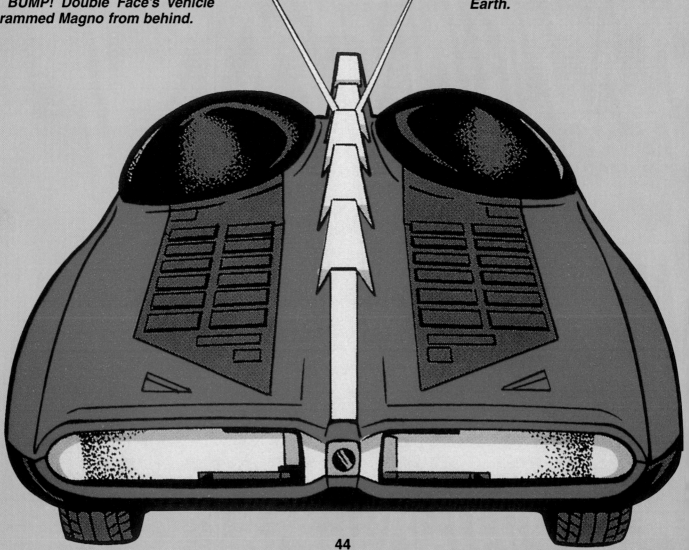

Gork planned for the poor, unsuspecting Stewarts to open the parcel, releasing the locust which would eat their house.

Without the protection of his human home, Dex would be out in the streets - an easy target for Count Dregon's forces!

In Spider Base, Dregon had walked up behind Gork who cringed away from him in fear.

"A good plan, but it failed! What went wrong?" snarled the Count.

"What went wrong? Telling would take too long!" insisted Gork.

Dregon would have none of it. "Continue or get bashed!" he threatened.

The alien reluctantly explained what happened. The huge parcel arrived at the Stewarts' house and the whole family came out to take a look.

"That cook book I ordered maybe?" said Barbara Stewart.

"A new toy for me!" hoped Albee Stewart.

Dex took a long, hard look at the massive, locust-shaped parcel.

"I'd say it was one of Count Dregon's Insectivores, probably a giant locust!"

The Stewart family were impressed. "You used your X-ray vision, right?" asked Mr. Stewart.

"I didn't need to," answered Dex. "The shape gave it away!"

"Oh, no!" cried the alien, as he finished his story. "I made a goof...Count Dregon will hit the roof!"

The seething Dregon grabbed hold of Gork and lifted him off the ground.

"Wrong, you clown! I'm not going to hit the roof - YOU ARE!"

Dregon hurled the latest failure

upwards. He bounced off the ceiling and fell back totally unconscious, landing in the middle of the conference table.

The table broke and thumped the head bad guy on the jaw.

Dregon was dazed. He staggered towards a frightened looking Cyclopter.

"Y-You're last to report...g-give me the bad news..."

Cyclopter nodded nervously and began to speak. "Right away, boss! I cleverly went underground to surprise the Masked Rider..."

An Insectivore had been selected to lead the attack, Cyclopter explained. The insect-like robot was a kind of burrowing beetle.

"Get digging!" Cyclopter ordered the Insectivore. "I want a tunnel dug from Spider Base to the Stewarts' house!"

DREGON'S DISASTERS!
Continuation...

The plan was for the tunnel to come out right underneath the home where Dex lived with his human friends.

"Then I shall lead a force of Commandoids along the tunnel, smash through the floor and capture the Masked Rider!" laughed Cyclopter.

Stage one of the plan worked perfectly. The tunnel was quickly dug by the Insectivore.

Cyclopter and a squad of Commandoids, Count Dregon's masked foot soldiers, then raced along the tunnel.

"Follow me to victory! Nothing can stop us now!" cried the one-eyed bad guy.

In the Spider Base, Count Dregon began tapping on the side of Cyclopter's head. There was a strangely hollow metallic sound.

"Hello? Hello? Is there anyone in there?" sneered Dregon. "Don't stop your story. I want to know the ending!"

The alien robot trembled and made a series of odd buzzing sounds.

Cyclopter explained that the tunnel finally reached a point underneath the Stewarts' house - or so he thought!

"Cease burrowing at once, Insectivore! Stand well back, Commandoids! The honour of gaining actual entry to the lair of the Masked Rider shall be mine!" Cyclopter announced loudly.

The alien robot with one eye began to dig. A few drops of water fell on his metal face.

"That's odd! How can it be raining inside a house?" asked a very puzzled Cyclopter.

It was not rain. The bad guys' tunnel was right underneath the boating lake!

"AYEEEEEEEEE!" shrieked Cyclopter as thousands of gallons of water filled the tunnel and swept away Cyclopter, Commandoids and Insectivore.

Count Dregon had fallen to his knees in Spider Base. He had buried his golden head in his hands and was sobbing uncontrollably.

"A whole Commandoid unit lost...a valuable Insectivore destroyed..."

Cyclopter unwisely butted in. "At least I survived!"

Dregon slowly stood up. He looked at Nefaria. Then Double Face. Next Gork. Finally Cyclopter. Every single one had failed him.

"You're all fired! Redundant! Sacked! Given the boot! You're out on your ears!" screeched the head bad guy.

Dregon's ex-followers left the main control room one by one. No-one said a word. They all knew there was no case for unfair dismissal.

Being unemployed bad guys was no fun. Maybe it was time for a change of career.

Nefaria thought about trying t become an actress and joinin the cast of 'Baywatch'.

Double Face considere running away and joining the ci cus.

Cyclopter always wanted to b a professional footballer.

Gork fancied going in t politics. Maybe even run for th White House.

The Count was alone in th control room. He neede replacement followers urgentl There was only one thing to do Advertise!

Local papers over the nex few days carried numerous larg advertisements. The potenti recruits to the ranks were aske to apply to Spider Base.

There was only one reply, bu the writer sounded just th person Dregon was looking for

The applicant had grea powers, which included supe strength and X-ray vision. H drove a powerful talking car an rode an equally powerful talkin motorbike.

"Perfect!" smiled Dregor "Now who is this from...?"

Then he saw the signature a the end of the joke letter: th Masked Rider!

Dregon knew he would have t re-hire his sacked followers.

"Better to have useless ba guys on my side than a supe hero good guy!" he moaned in sad sort of way!

WIN A TALKING CAR OR BIKE!

IT'S competition time, as we give you a chance to win a super Masked Rider toy, from Bandai! The first prize winner in this easy-to-enter competition will win a super Magno talking car! The car comes complete with two phrases and power claws that can grab up Mutant Marauders! The second and third prize winners will each receive a Masked Rider talking bike, each with its own signature phrase or sound effect.

Just answer the three easy questions and send a postcard to the address shown below!

Take a look at the picture above. It is taken from one of the all-action Masked Rider picture-strips in this Annual. What is the name of the story in which this drawing appears?

The above picture is from another picture-strip in this book. One word has been removed from what the Masked Rider is saying. Can you find the original to find the missing word?

Which of these statements, relating to Ferbus, is true? (a) Ferbus is a teddy bear who came to life; (b) Ferbus is from the same planet as the Masked Rider; (c) Ferbus is a robot.

When you have answered each of the three questions, write the answers on the back of a postcard, or the back of an empty, sealed envelope. Add your name, age and address and send your entry to: Masked Rider Competition, Grandreams Ltd., Jadwin House, 205/211 Kentish Town Road, London NW5 2JU. The closing date for all entries is 31st March, 1997. The three prizes will go to the senders of the three correct entries drawn from the postbag. The Publisher's decision will be final.

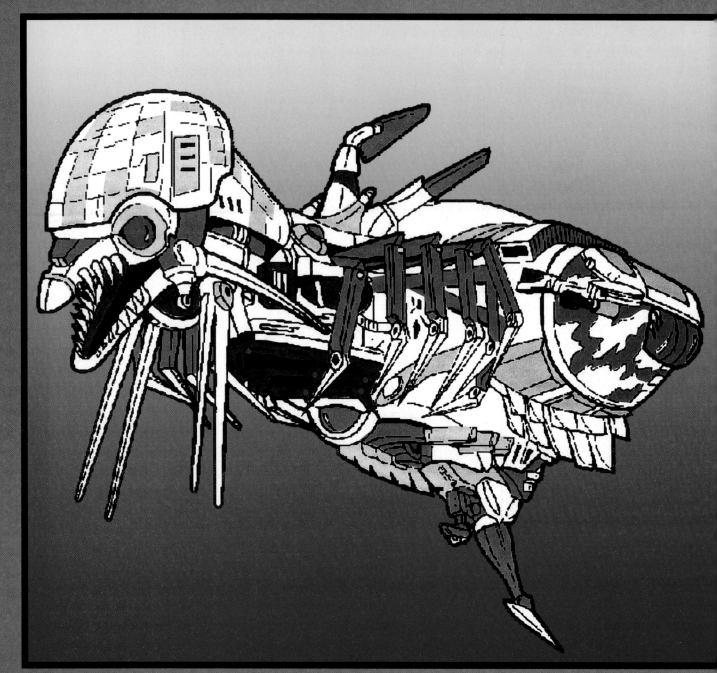

SPIDER BASE!

CLASSIFIED INFORMATION
Spider Base is the sinister lair of Count Dregon and his freakish followers, including Nefaria, Gork, Cyclopter and Double Face. It's location is always kept secret!

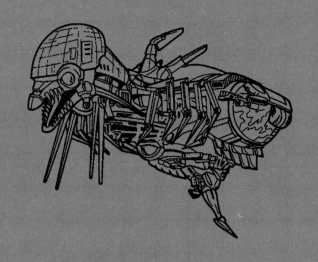

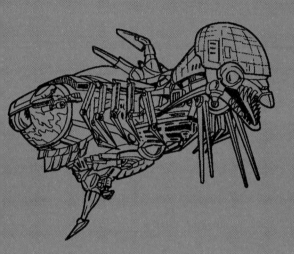

Heavily armed with a wide array of weapons and armoured against enemy attacks, the Spider Base is capable of landing virtually anywhere. It can operate on land, in the air or even in deep space!

Count Dregon has fitted cutting and digging devices to Spider Base, for use in attack situations. See the use of the drill in the 'Day of the Volcano' story, earlier in this Masked Rider Annual.

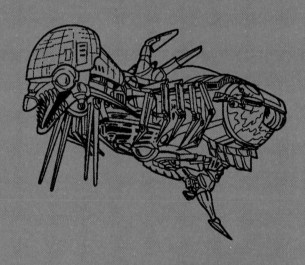

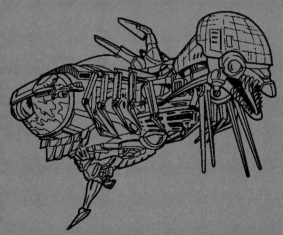

From Spider Base, Count Dregon sends out his army of Insectivores to devastate our world. Perhaps, one day, the Masked Rider will manage to find Spider Base and put it out of action. Let's hope so!

COVER STORY

WARNING!

COUNT DREGON HAS SABOTAGED THE INFORMATION IN THIS STORY, BY CAUSING SIX MISTAKES TO APPEAR. FIND THEM TO DEFEAT THE BAD GUY!

SHA-DOOOOM! Another building blew apart as a jet of liquid flame hit home! The city was in chaos, under attack from the dreaded forces of the evil Countess Dregon!

"Next target, Insectivore!" ordered the one-eyed robot known as Cyclopter. "Singe the city library! Make it burn!"

Dregon's Insectivore machine, a giant fire-breathing ant, obeyed Cyclopter. It opened its mouth and fired a fiery jet which sent the city library up in flames.

Cyclopter laughed his mechanical laugh. He knew the Masked Rider would soon arrive to try and be a hero. Then the Insectivore fire ant would destroy him once and for all.

Or that was the plan. It started to go wrong the moment the Masked Rider, on his Combat Hopper motorbike, surprised Cyclopter by jumping right through a wall of flame!

"Electro Saber Activate!" roared the super hero as he sailed through the air, swinging his sword-like weapon above his head.

The robot waved his arms helplessly and fell over backwards. Being a good guy, the Masked Rider made sure he missed landing on the machine.

"Boy! That was fun!" said the talking bike. "Can we do it again?"

The Masked Rider smiled behind his mask. "Not right now, buddy! We've a city to save and an Insectivore to beat!"

Cyclopter kept down as he saw the grandson of Lord Lexian race off towards the fire-breathing ant. This was one battle the robot wanted to keep well clear of.

FWOOSSSH! The Insectivore ant fired another jet of fire. The force of the flames knocked the super hero off his machine. He landed in a heap on the ground as the menacing Insectivore closed in.

ZAP! The motorbike fired a powerful energy beam at the Insectivore, blowing a huge hole in its side and slowing the machine for vital seconds.

"Catch a Rider Kick, ugly bug!" cried the super hero, as he launched a devastating flying kick against the head of the charging Insectivore.

SNAP! The machine's head broke off and sailed away through the air.

"That mechanical monstrosity really lost its head, Tex!" laughed the talking motorbike.

There was no time for his master to see the funny side. The headless body of the Insectivore was trying to run him down.

ZUUNK! The super hero hurled his Electro Saber at his nightmarish attacker. The weapon slammed into the back of the machine - but it kept on coming!

The Prince from Egenoi turned and ran, leading the robot horror towards the nearest blazing building. He jumped clear just as the whole structure collapsed, burying the Insectivore beetle for good.

"Help!" cried Cyclopter as the Masked Rider's motorbike chased him away. The robot's circuits trembled. He knew Dregon would punish him for his failure.

With the Insectivore danger over, the emergency services could finally put out the fires. The people clapped and cheered. Their city was safe again. Thanks to the Masked Rider!

ANSWERS:

1. Count Dregon, not Countess Dregon; 2. Combat Chopper, not Combat Hopper; 3. King Lexian, not Lord Lexian; 4. The Masked Rider is Dex, not Tex; 5. He is the Prince from Edenoi, not the Prince from Egenoi; 6. The Insectivore was an ant, not a beetle.

SABAN'S
MASKED RIDER™

QUIZ TIME

1 Double Face is the most bizarre of Count Dregon's fiendish followers. Do you know the military rank of this two-faced alien? He's not a sergeant. Not a corporal. Which of the following ranks is he?
(a) A Colonel?
(b) An Admiral? (c) A General?

2 105 per cent hero! The picture on the right shows super fit Dex taking part in some athletics at his high school. What is the name of the school?
(a) Bellwood High?
(b) Leawood High?
(c) Larwood High?

3 When Dex wears his Masked Rider Super Gold outfit, he rides his super fast and super powerful talking motorbike called Ultra Chopper. Is this true or false?

4 What is the name of Dex's fur ball alien pet which followed him from the planet Edenoi?
(a) Ferbus?
(b) Furbus?
(c) Ferbos?

5 Here is a rare picture of Dex with some of his friends on his home planet. Are the power-giving crystals on their foreheads called Mind Crystals or Brain Crystals?

6 Count Dregon is the nasty alien tyrant who was banished from Edenoi by King Lexian. Now Dregon is up to no good on Earth. Do you know what relation Count Dregon is to the Masked Rider? Is he...?
(a) His father?
(b) His brother? (c) His uncle?

7 15-year-old Molly, left, is the adopted daughter of the Stewart family. Can you name the family's adopted son?
(a) Albert?
(b) Albee?
(c) Alfred?

8 Dex transforms into his super hero identity as the insect-like Masked Rider by shouting out 'Ectophase Activate' to call up his special powers. Is this true or false?

ANSWERS

1.(c); 2. (b); 3. False. It's the Super Chopper bike with the Super Gold outfit; 4. (a); 5. They are called 'Mind Crystals'; 6. (c); 7. (b); 8.True.

Finally, it's...
FERBUS!

LALI, LALI!

TRANSLATION BY *DEX*

GRRRRR! This is one very angry Ferbus speaking! These are the last pages of this annual and only now does the Masked Rider's fur ball pet (that's me!) finally get some space to himself! It's not fair, is it?

My words are being translated for you by my master, Dex. On the left is a fantastically brilliant picture of super-intelligent me. Am I not very handsome? 'Lali, lali' is part of my own alien language. It means 'Hello' in your funny Earth language.

Dex and I live with the Stewart family: Hal, Barbara, Molly and Albee. They all like me a lot (they have very good taste!) although Mr Stewart is allergic to fur (funny man!).

Barbara Stewart runs a busy catering business from home. Her yummy chocolate cakes often go missing. It's not my fault - I have a very sweet tooth!

I love eating sugar, but it makes poor me bounce off walls like a furry ping pong ball. Not many people know that!

On the next page are more pictures of a very handsome fur ball (that's me!). Enjoy them!